Poké

I want to be the very best the...
To beat all the rest, yeah, tha...

Catch 'em, Catch 'em, Gotta catch 'em all

Pokémon I'll search across the land
Look far and wide
Release from my hand
The power that's inside

Catch 'em, Catch 'em, Gotta catch 'em all Pokémon!

Gotta catch 'em all, Gotta catch 'em all
Gotta catch 'em all, Gotta catch 'em all

At least one hundred and fifty or more to see
To be a Pokémon Master is my destiny

Catch 'em, Catch 'em, Gotta catch 'em all
Gotta catch 'em all, Pokémon! (repeat three times)

Can YOU Rap all 150?

Here's the next 32 Pokémon.
Catch the next book *Battle for the Zephyr Badge*
for more of the Poke Rap.

Articuno, Jynx, Nidorina, Beedrill
Haunter, Squirtle, Chansey,
Parasect, Exeggcute, Muk, Dewgong
Pidgeotto, Lapras, Vulpix, Rhydon

Charizard, Machamp, Pinsir, Koffing
Dugtrio, Golbat, Staryu, Magikarp
Ninetales, Ekans, Omastar
Scyther, Tentacool, Dragonair, Magmar

Words and Music by Tamara Loeffler and John Siegler
Copyright © 1999 Pikachu Music (BMI)
Worldwide rights for Pikachu Music administered by Cherry River Music Co. (BMI)
All Rights Reserved   Used by Permission

Collect them all!

Prepare for Trouble

All rights reserved. Published by Scholastic Inc., *Publishers since 1920*. SCHOLASTIC and associated logos are trademarks and/or registered trademarks of Scholastic Inc.

The publisher does not have any control over and does not assume any responsibility for author or third-party websites or their content.

This book is a work of fiction. Names, characters, places, and incidents are either the product of the author's imagination or are used fictitiously, and any resemblance to actual persons, living or dead, business establishments, events, or locales is entirely coincidental.

ISBN 978-1-338-28404-1

10 9 8 7 6 5 4 3 2 1   18 19 20 21 22

Printed in the U.S.A.   40
First printing 2018

Adapted by Tracey West

Scholastic Inc.

Sun, Sand, and Shellder

Even bad guys need a vacation.

And when it came to bad guys, no one was badder than Jessie, James, and Meowth.

Jessie was a girl with long red hair and a short, fiery temper.

James was a purple-haired boy who was great at concocting evil schemes – and even better at messing them up.

Meowth was a clever Pokémon who helped them cause trouble.

The three villains worked for Team Rocket, a powerful crime organization. Team Rocket's leader, Giovanni, was bent on capturing the world's rarest Pokémon.

Today, however, Giovanni was bent on capturing the sun's rays. He lounged on a beach on Seafoam Island. His Persian, a sleek, Classy Cat Pokémon, purred at his side.

Jessie, James, and Meowth were on the beach, too. But they weren't lounging in the sun. They were digging in the wet sand. Everyone else on the beach wore bathing suits, but they were stuck in their white Team Rocket uniforms.

Meowth jealously watched Giovanni stroke Persian's sleek fur. "Just look how the Boss fawns over that feline fink," Meowth grumbled.

James tossed his shovel aside. "Some vacation this turned out to be," he complained. "First the Boss has us swabbing the deck of his yacht. Now he's got us digging for clams like a couple of clam diggers. Well, I've just dug my last dig!"

Meowth pushed the shovel back into James's hand. "Ya better keep digging until we get to China, or else he'll make us take another pay cut," Meowth warned.

Jessie frowned and turned to James. "Why don't we bury Meowth in the sand headfirst?" she suggested.

"Hey!" Meowth cried.

Just then, the sound of laughter drifted over the ocean waves. Happy people surfed, swam, and water-skied in the sparkling blue sea.

"Everybody's having fun but us!" James whined. "The Boss makes me so mad sometimes." James angrily slammed his shovel into the sand. The shovel became a blur as he furiously dug and dug. Sand flew everywhere.

Thump! James's shovel hit something hard.

"Jess, I think I discovered a colossal clam!" James exclaimed. He dug away the sand to reveal a large blue-gray shell.

Suddenly, the shell flew up from the hole and landed in front of them. This was no ordinary shell. It was a Water-type Pokémon.

"Look, it's a Shellder!" said Jessie.

Two round white eyes stared out from inside the Pokémon's shell. Shellder stuck out its long pink tongue. "Oh, you're a wise guy, huh?" said Meowth. "Don't stick that tongue out at me, ya crummy crustacean, or I'll clam you up good!"

4

"We need less talk and more action," said James. He threw a red-and-white Poké Ball into the air. "Weezing, I choose you!"

"'I choose you'? You sound like that little twerp," Jessie said. She was thinking of Ash Ketchum, a Pokémon Trainer from Pallet Town who was always spoiling their plans.

"I just wanted to see what it was like to be in his Goody Two-Shoes," James joked.

Weezing popped out of the ball. The Pokémon

looked like a purple cloud with two heads. Weezing was known for its powerful poison attacks.

Weezing whizzed through the air, aiming to slam into Shellder. The Water-type Pokémon slammed back hard. Weezing reeled, weakened from the attack.

"Poor Weezing just got shell-shocked!" said Meowth.

Shellder jumped right in with another attack. A blue beam shot out of its shell.

"Look, that's an Ice Beam!" said Jessie. "You might end up with a freezing Weezing!"

But Weezing dodged the beam just in time.

"Weezing, use your Haze attack!" James said quickly.

Thick black smoke poured from Weezing's body. The smoke quickly engulfed the Shellder. One puff of the poison was all it took. Shellder rolled back on the sand in a faint.

Jessie threw out a Poké Ball. "Come to Jessie, Shellder!"

A red light shot out of the Poké Ball. The light hit Shellder, and the Water-type Pokémon disappeared inside the ball.

"Nice capture!" Jessie said proudly.

"Hey, that's not fair," James said. "Weezing is my Pokémon. I should be the one to get Shellder."

"Finders keepers," replied Jessie.

Before their argument could turn into a full-fledged fight, a Team Rocket soldier dressed in black stepped between them.

"Get a grip, you clowns," said the soldier. "The Boss wants to see you right away!"

Obey the Boss
. . . or Else!

Giovanni looked at Jessie, James, and Meowth through his dark sunglasses. Beside him, his Persian stared at them with cold, slanted eyes.

Jessie, James, and Meowth may have complained about Giovanni behind his back. But now they tried hard to get on his good side.

"Thanks for letting us dig around for clams, boss," James said.

"Yeah," said Meowth. "We really dig it!"

"In fact," said Jessie, "we dug up something very

special for you." She reached for the Poké Ball that held Shellder.

"Not right now," growled Giovanni. "I'm sick and tired of watching you three blundering fools. You never do anything right!"

Jessie, James, and Meowth hung their heads in shame.

"I've got a simple job for you," said Giovanni. "And considering how simple-minded you are, you should be perfect for it."

"What is it, Boss?" asked Jessie. "We'll do anything."

"I want you to break into the laboratory of the famous

Professor Westwood," Giovanni said.

"Famous? I've never heard of him," James piped up.

Jessie nudged him with her elbow.

Giovanni sighed. "Of course not. I should have known better. Professor Westwood programmed the Pokédex."

Jessie nodded. The Pokédex was a handheld computer that contained information about the world's Pokémon.

"I'll bet Westwood's place is loaded with Pokémon," James said. "Boss, consider it done!"

"Looting laboratories is one of our specialties," Jessie added.

Giovanni leaned forward. "You'd better not mess this one up," he said. "Or else!"

"Or else what?" asked James.

There was a cold silence. "Do you really want to know?" Giovanni asked.

"Of course not," Jessie said. She and Meowth quickly grabbed James and dragged him away. "We won't let you down!"

Soon they were hiding behind a sand dune, scoping out Professor Westwood's lab.

"This is our big chance," said Meowth. "If we do this right, our clam-digging days will be over. Instead of that pitiful Persian, we'll be the ones living in style."

"First we have to break in," Jessie said, looking through her binoculars. "That's going to be tricky."

Professor Westwood's lab was a large concrete building that sat on a hill above the beach. The bottom of the building seemed to be windowless. On the very top, there was a dome that seemed to be open on all sides.

"We have to get up there," James said. "But how?"

Just then, a shadow passed over them. They looked up. A boy in a bathing suit was parasailing over the beach. He held on to a harness attached to a parachute. The harness was attached to a cable, and the cable was attached to a speedboat that pulled the parachute along. Wind billowed under the parachute, keeping the boy aloft.

Meowth grinned. "I think we found our answer!"

Jessie, James, and Meowth scraped together the last of their money to rent a parasail. They strapped themselves into the harness. Then they told the boat's driver to take them past Professor Westwood's lab.

The parasail took off, lifting Team Rocket high in the sky.

"Breaking into this lab will be a snap," Jessie said as they got closer to the laboratory.

"And it looks like Professor Westwood's waiting for us. How nice!" said James. He could make out a chubby man wearing a lab coat on the roof.

"He's not the only one," Meowth said. "There's a kid with dark hair and a baseball cap. And a girl with orange hair. And another kid with spiky hair."

"I see them," said Jessie. "There's even a little yellow Poké – oh, no!"

"Are you thinking what I'm thinking?" Meowth asked.

"It's that little twerp Ash and his funny-looking friends," Jessie snapped.

"No fair!" James cried. "He's always showing up when we don't want him to. It's his fault we mess everything up, not ours."

"We can handle him," Jessie said. "He'll be so impressed by our fantastic entrance, he won't know what to do."

"Uh, Jessie," Meowth said. "I think we're going to −"

Crash! The parasail slammed into the top of the dome. The harness broke off, and Jessie, James, and Meowth tumbled to the roof of the lab. The parachute covered them like a blanket.

Jessie was determined to make an impressive entrance.

"Prepare for trouble!" she yelled from under the parachute.

"Make it double," said James weakly.

They recited the Team Rocket motto as they tried to untangle themselves from the cloth.

To protect the world from devastation,

To unite all peoples within our nation.

To denounce the evils of truth and love,

To extend our reach to the stars above!

"Jessie!" Jessie cried, finally free.

"James!" James stepped free, too.

"Team Rocket! Blast off at the speed of light! Surrender now or prepare to fight," they finished.

"Meowth! That's right!" added Meowth, popping out from under the parachute.

Ash Ketchum looked shocked. "What are you guys doing here?" he asked.

Jessie laughed. "We're bad guys. We're here to do bad stuff, of course. And you can't stop us!"

Psy-bro?

Ash and his friends looked stunned. Misty, the girl with the orange hair, held a small Pokémon in her arms. Togepi had hatched from an egg. It still wore the colorful shell around its body.

Next to Misty stood a tall boy with dark hair. Brock had been hanging around Ash for almost as long as Team Rocket could remember.

The little yellow Pokémon, of course, was Ash's Pikachu. The Electric-type Pokémon had pointy ears and a lightning-bolt-shaped tail.

Sparks danced on its red cheeks as Pikachu angrily glared at Team Rocket.

Normally, Team Rocket would have tried to swipe Pikachu right away. But today they had another mission.

Jessie faced Professor Westwood. Tufts of gray hair stuck out from either side of his bald head.

"Are you Professor Westwood, the man who programmed the Pokédex?" Jessie asked him.

"Yes, I am," Westwood replied nervously.

"Well, now you're gonna program the Team Rocke-dex!" James said. "We'll give you all the vital statistics you need."

Jessie handed Professor Westwood a piece of paper.

The professor read aloud. "'Jessie, the beautiful female member of the team. Her brilliant mind is surpassed only by her style and personality.'"

Jessie struck a glamorous pose.

The professor read on. "'James, with the looks of a movie star, the agility of an Olympic athlete . . . and a head that's too small for his brain'?"

James flexed his muscles like a body-builder. "That's me!"

Westwood continued. "'And Meowth — Team Rocket's feline mastermind whose diabolically clever plans never fail. The only thing sharper than its mind are its claws.'"

Meowth took a little bow. "I'm also humble, and I'm housebroken!"

Misty grabbed the paper from Professor Westwood. "It's all lies!" she protested.

"You'll see that we're telling the truth," Jessie said, "when we complete our brilliant plan and steal all of the Pokémon in this lab!"

Professor Westwood looked puzzled. "But that Slowpoke over there is the only Pokémon I've got." He pointed to a spot in the corner.

Team Rocket looked. A large pink Pokémon that looked like a hippo sat there, staring blankly into the air. Its long tail curled around its chubby legs.

"A Slowpoke?" James asked. "Are you sure you don't have anything a little smarter?"

Slowpoke stood up. Then it plodded over to Professor Westwood on four legs. *"Slowwwwwwwwwwwww-ww . . . poooooooooooooooooooooooooooke."* It seemed to take forever for the Pokémon to get out the word.

Meowth nudged Jessie. "Ya still got that Shellder we caught?" Meowth asked.

Jessie nodded.

Meowth huddled with Jessie and James. "You're right. It ain't too bright, but when we get through with it, the Boss'll be in for a big surprise! We can use that Shellder to make Slowpoke evolve into Slowbro."

Jessie grinned. She threw out a Poké Ball, and the Shellder appeared in a blaze of light. Shellder stuck out its tongue.

"What a brilliant idea!" Jessie said. "We've got something to make Slowpoke evolve with one itty-bitty bite."

"All Shellder has to do is chomp down on Slowpoke's tail," Meowth explained. "Then Slowpoke will evolve into Slowbro. That's one Pokémon we can bring back to the Boss."

Professor Westwood looked alarmed. "Oh, you can't do that! I've been studying Slowpoke to find out why it evolves when Shellder bites on its tail. If you take it, all my research will be ruined!"

"We said we were bad guys, remember?" Jessie said. "Shellder, chomp away!"

Westwood pushed the pink Pokémon. "Slowpoke, hurry up! Get out of here!"

"Slowwwww . . . poooooooooke." Slowpoke took one very slow step.

Frustrated, Professor Westwood picked up Slowpoke and ran through an open door.

"After him!" Jessie cried.

Westwood seemed to have superhuman strength as he carried the heavy Pokémon down the stairs and out onto the beach. Team Rocket followed right behind, and Ash and his friends were right next to them.

Finally the professor dropped Slowpoke onto the sand. He tried to push Slowpoke into the water, but the Pokémon wouldn't budge.

Shellder hopped down the beach.

"Shellder, go!" Jessie yelled. "Chomp that Slowpoke!"

Ash ran in front of Slowpoke. "Leave that Slowpoke alone!" he cried. He reached for a Poké Ball, ready to battle if he had to.

Misty held up a Poké Ball. "I can handle this, Ash," she said. "We're near the ocean and Water-type Pokémon are my specialty. Staryu, I choose you!"

Team Rocket held its breath, waiting for the powerful starfish-shaped Pokémon to appear. Jessie knew that Staryu could do a lot of damage to a Pokémon like Shellder.

A white light flashed . . .

. . . and an orange Pokémon that looked like a duck appeared.

"Psyduck!" Misty wailed. "You weren't supposed to come out."

Jessie grinned. "Looks like we've got the edge in this battle."

Psyduck faced Slowpoke. The two Pokémon stared at each other. They started to greet each other in Pokémon language.

"*Psy . . .*"

"*Slowwww . . .*"

"*. . . duck.*"

"*. . . poooooke.*"

Jessie rolled her eyes. "Shellder, break up this pitiful party!"

Shellder hopped up and chomped down on a tail . . . Psyduck's tail!

"*Psy! Psy!*" Psyduck cried.

"Hey, it's a Psy-bro!" Ash joked.

Jessie frowned. "Shellder, you've got the wrong Pokémon. Get off Psyduck and take a bite out of Slowpoke!"

Psyduck beat Shellder to the punch. Psyduck wiggled its feathered tail. Shellder went flying through the air and landed in Jessie's arms.

"Hey, Psyduck used its Tail Whip," Misty said proudly. "Not bad, Psyduck."

James threw a Poké Ball. "Weezing, make sure that Psyduck is permanently quacked up!"

Slowpoke Showdown

A foul smell filled the air as the purple Poison Gas Pokémon popped out of its Poké Ball. Weezing flew over to Psyduck and started bouncing on its head. Psyduck tried to run away, but it fell into the sand.

"What did I expect? Psyduck's got two left webbed feet," Misty moaned.

Jessie made her move. "Shellder, clamp onto Slowpoke's tail now!" she yelled. She threw Shellder as hard as she could.

Shellder flew across the beach . . .

. . . and landed right on Psyduck's head!

Jessie sighed.

Psyduck sat up. It grabbed its head with its wings.

"All right!" Misty said. "Psyduck's getting a headache. Now it can use its most powerful attacks."

Psyduck's white eyes started to glow with blue light. The Duck Pokémon aimed the light at Jessie, James, Meowth, and Weezing.

"Weezing, stop that dim witted duck!" James yelled.

Weezing tried to fly through the air, but it didn't move an inch.

"I can't move, either!" Jessie cried. "My whole body's stuck."

James and Meowth were frozen in place, too.

"Nice Disable attack, Psyduck!" Misty cheered.

The blue light grew brighter. It surrounded Team Rocket. Suddenly, the bad guys found themselves being lifted up into the air. Psyduck's attack sent them flying across the beach.

"Oh, no! We can't be blasting off already," James moaned.

Thud! Team Rocket landed in the sand.

Meowth spit some sand out of its mouth. "We're not out of this yet! I'm not going back to the Boss without a Slowbro."

Meowth ran back down the beach. Jessie and James followed.

"Shellder, it's time to take a bite out of that Slowpoke!" Jessie shouted as they reached Ash and the others.

"Shellder's one step ahead of you," Ash told them.

Ash was right. It was happening so fast. First, Slowpoke accidentally bopped Shellder on the head with its tail. That caused Shellder to open up its shell and clamp down hard on Slowpoke's tail.

Within seconds, Slowpoke and Shellder were bathed in white light. The light got brighter and brighter. Jessie, James, and Meowth shaded their eyes.

Then suddenly, the light faded. Slowpoke and Shellder had transformed.

Now Slowpoke stood upright on two feet. The Shellder on its tail had changed shape, so that it looked like a spiral.

"Wow! Slowpoke and Shellder evolved into Slowbro," Ash said.

"I finally understand!" cried Professor Westwood. "Shellder and Slowpoke evolve together because it helps them both."

"What do you mean, Professor?" Brock asked.

"Shellder helps balance Slowpoke, so Slowpoke can stand on two legs and use more effective attacks," said Professor Westwood. "And the Shellder benefits because now it can travel around on land."

"That's all fascinating," Jessie said dryly. "We'll be sure to tell the Boss — while we're handing over this Slowbro."

Jessie, James, Meowth, and Weezing charged at the Slowbro like an advancing army.

"Uh, Professor, did you say something about Slowbro having effective attacks?" Brock asked.

Professor Westwood's eyes widened. "Of course. Slowbro, Mega Punch!"

Jessie, James, and Meowth advanced on Slowbro. It was almost within Team Rocket's grasp.

Then Slowbro pulled back its right arm. Its fist began to pulsate with energy.

"What's happening?" James asked.

Pow! Slowbro's fist slammed into James. The punch sent the Pokémon thief flying.

Pow! Pow! Pow! Jessie, Meowth, and Weezing all fell victim to the Mega Punch.

Thud! They flew across the island and landed in the sand once again.

"What just happened?" James asked as he tried to sit up.

"Isn't it obvious? You've failed once again," a cool voice said.

Jessie, James, and Meowth sat up. They had landed on the beach right next to Giovanni's lounge chair. Persian sat at Giovanni's side, a sly smile on its face.

"Uh, we broke into the lab, Boss, just like you asked!" Meowth said.

"And we got you a Slowbro," said Jessie.

"Only we don't have it anymore because that little twerp Ash Ketchum showed up and ruined everything, just like he always does," added James.

"I've had enough of your excuses!" Giovanni thundered. "You're going to have to earn back my trust if you want to keep wearing those Team Rocket uniforms."

"Anything, Boss!" Meowth said. "We'll do anything!"

"I need you to go on an errand," Giovanni said. "I have commissioned a jeweler in the Savage Mountains to make a collar for my Persian. I need you to fetch it for me."

"Perrrrrrrrr," purred the Persian.

"Meowth fetches nothing for a Persian!" Meowth said.

Jessie clamped a hand over Meowth's mouth.

"No problem, Boss," Jessie said. "Consider it done."

Giovanni and Persian turned and walked away.

Meowth flopped down into the sand. "This is awful. No one gets out of the Savage Mountains alive. We couldn't sink any lower. We're failures!"

"You're right, Meowth." James hugged Meowth, and they both sobbed.

Jessie stood up. "We are not failures," she said. "We'll do this job. Then we'll go back to being the Boss's favorites. Remember the time we rounded up a whole school of Magikarp? We weren't failures then."

"I'm not sure I remember," said James.

"Let's go get our hot-air balloon and head to the Savage Mountains," Jessie said. "I'll tell you the story on the way. It happened in the Orange Islands. We were following Ash, trying to capture Pikachu. . . ."

5

Magikarp Capture

"Ash and Misty were with that other friend of theirs," Jessie said. "That guy with the green shorts."

"I think his name's Tracey," Meowth said. "He's a Pokémon Watcher."

"Well, that day we were the ones watching them," Jessie said. "We were perched in a palm tree on Tankan Island. Ash and his friends were talking with a man in a safari uniform. They were studying a stream.

"At first I thought that staring at water was what twerps did for fun. But I was wrong. Soon hundreds of Magikarp came swimming up the stream. The water was filled with the orange Fish Pokémon."

"I remember," said Meowth, licking its lips. "There were Magikarp everywhere! That stream was swimming with future fishsticks."

"You may have thought of them as snack food, but I saw their true potential," Jessie reminded Meowth. "I knew that Magikarp are worthless, no matter how many there are. But Magikarp evolve into Gyarados."

James got a dreamy look in his eyes. "Gyarados. The huge Water- and Flying-type Pokémon strike fear into the hearts of everyone who sees them. They are blue and ferocious. Their fangs can crush stones, and their scales are harder than steel." He sighed. "The Boss would give a big reward to anyone who brought him a Gyarados."

"Exactly!" Jessie said. "That's why I came up with my plan. We could capture all the Magikarp before they evolved, because capturing Magikarp is much easier than capturing Gyarados. Then when they evolved, we'd have an unstoppable army of Gyarados!

"You both agreed that my plan was brilliant. We followed the Magikarp to a large lake on the island. Then we waited until nightfall. We charged up our Magikarp-shaped submarine and crept in the dark lake waters.

"Then we made our move. We activated the mechanical arms on the submarine. The arms scooped up scores of sleeping Magikarp. They shoved the

Magikarp in through the mouth of the submarine. Soon the sub was filled with flipping, flopping Magikarp. Our Gyarados army was born!"

Jessie turned to James and Meowth. "So you see," she told them, "we didn't fail that time."

Meowth scowled. "Gee, Jess. Don't ya remember? Our Magikarp capture ended up in a mega-mess!"

"I don't know what you're talking about," Jessie replied.

"Then let me finish the story," Meowth said.

6

Revenge
of the Gyarados

"We did catch a lot of Magikarp that day," Meowth began. "Too many Magikarp. Our submarine started to sink faster than a Snorlax in quicksand."

"That's right," James added. "I started tossing some of the Magikarp out of the sub. That saved us from sinking. We rose to the surface of the lake."

"Hey, I'm telling this story!" Meowth interrupted.

"Sorry," James said.

"Anyway," Meowth continued. "We still had plenty of Magikarp left. But our troubles weren't over. When we climbed out of the sub, we saw Ash and his friends on the shore of the lake. They were pretty steamed about us trying to steal those Magikarp.

"That's when I came up with a perfect plan. We started throwing the Magikarp to Ash and his friends. They didn't want the floppy fish to hit land, so soon their arms were filled with Magikarp. And that left us free to steal Pikachu.

"I activated the mechanical arm, and it reached out and plopped Pikachu into a glass cage. James took the cage from the arm and held on tight. That little Mouse Pokémon pounded with all its might, but it couldn't escape.

"Pikachu thought about giving us a little shock, but

Ash reminded it that the Magikarp would be shocked, too," Meowth said.

"Maybe that little twerp has a brain after all," James remarked.

Meowth continued. "Ash mighta been using his brain that day, because he called on his Bulbasaur – you know,

that Seed Pokémon that looks like a tulip. Bulbasaur opened up the green bulb on its back and some nasty vines shot out."

"I remember," James said. "Those vicious vines hurt! I lost my grip on Pikachu."

"That's right," said Meowth. "Luckily, I caught Pikachu. Then Bulbasaur aimed its vines at me, so I threw it to Jessie."

"I caught Pikachu next," Jessie said. "Bulbasaur tried to whip me with its vines, but I dodged out of the way. Pikachu was ours!"

"Only for a minute," Meowth continued. "When James got hit by the vines, he fell headfirst into a Magikarp. One of those fishy freaks chomped on James's head."

James shuddered. "It was awful. I thought I was a goner," James said. "Besides, it was really messing up my hair."

"Jessie and I tried to yank that Magikarp off you," Meowth said. "While we were distracted, Ash swiped Pikachu back from Jessie."

"I really don't remember that part at all," Jessie sniffed.

"Then disaster struck," Meowth continued. "The Magikarp all started to glow with an eerie light. The light got so bright, I had to cover my eyes. It seemed to fill up the whole lake.

"The Magikarp were evolving! The water in the lake began to churn. A whirlpool rose up — and we were on top of it! We blasted off into the night. When we came to, we were surrounded by angry Gyarados."

James shivered. "How did we get away from them, anyway?"

"That's not important," Meowth said. "What is important is that this story proves we're failures. We might as well go fetch that collar for the Boss's Persian. We're not fit to do anything else."

James stared at his black boots. Jessie didn't say anything for a while.

She finally spoke. "I don't care what you say. We're not failures," she said. "But you're right about one thing. We should head for the Savage Mountains. It's the only way to make the Boss happy."

James and Meowth agreed. The three Pokémon thieves hopped into their hot-air balloon. It was decorated with a Meowth face.

The wind was fast and strong, and they soon found themselves sailing across the sky. In the distance, they could see a jagged mountain range. The mountains' peaks looked like sharp teeth pointed at the clouds.

"There they are," Meowth said. "The Savage Mountains."

"They don't look so tough," James said.

"Of course. They're no match for Team Rocket!" Jessie added.

A cheerful mood overtook the Pokémon thieves. They got comfortable in the balloon basket, ready to relax.

Then, suddenly, the sky became dark.

Jessie stood up. "What's this?" she asked.

Thick black storm clouds gathered in the sky. The wind kicked up.

"Just a little storm," Meowth said. "It'll pass."

"I'm not so sure," James said, pointing.

The storm was centered over the Savage Mountains. Angry streaks of lightning lit up the mountain tops. Deep thunder boomed in the distance.

"*Meowth!* We're headed right for it!" Meowth cried.

Icy rain poured from the clouds. Jessie, James, and Meowth huddled together in a corner of the basket.

"We're not going to make it!" James wailed as

the balloon rocked in the winds. "We're going to get smashed to smithereens!"

"Get a grip, James," Jessie said crossly.

"Our life of crime has led us to this," James said. "Maybe we should try to get honest work."

"Did you say work?" Meowth asked. "This rain must be short-circuiting your brain."

"It's not such a crazy idea," James said. "We've been paid to work before. Remember that time we were called in to round up those Electrode. . . ."

The Electrode Eliminator

"It all started when we were traveling around the Orange Islands," James began. "I overheard a conversation between two men from Hamlin Island. They said they had to flee their island because it was swarming with Electrode. And since Electrode can explode easily, that didn't make the people of Hamlin too happy. The Electrode kept blowing up all over the place. Something had to be done to stop them.

"They hired a Diglett rancher to handle the problem," James continued. "He was using the Diglett to round up the Electrode."

Jessie snickered. "Ridiculous! Diglett are nothing but overgrown worms with big noses. Who would use them to stand up against powerful Pokémon like Electrode?"

"We all thought it was ridiculous," James said. "Especially the people of Hamlin Island. That's why they hired us as soon as I assured them that we could wipe out the Electrode in no time."

Meowth got a dreamy look in its eyes. "They threw tons of money at us. I'll never forget that! Beautiful, beautiful money."

"Of course, James spent it all on his Electrode Eliminator," Jessie grumbled.

Now it was James's turn to get a dreamy look. "It was the finest machine I've ever built. A real masterpiece. First, I constructed a giant tank so we could travel the streets safely. Then I added two giant arms made of a special alloy. When the arms smashed down on the Electrode, the Pokémon would explode. Exploding makes Electrode weak. Then we could pick them up and dump them in a special holding compartment on the back of the tank.

"It was the perfect plan. When I finished the machine, we climbed inside the tank. Then we charged down the streets of Hamlin Island," James said.

"Those streets were crawling with Electrode," Meowth remembered.

"We were about to start pounding away," James continued, "when that little twerp Ash interfered. He and his friends were in town, helping the Diglett rancher.

"But there was nothing they could do to stop us. My Electrode Eliminator was too powerful. The mechanical arms whacked the Electrode one by one. *Bam! Bam! Bam!* The explosions rocked the streets.

"It was a snap to scoop up the weakened Electrode. The arms grabbed them and started throwing them into the tank," James said. "Then suddenly, everything got quiet. We stuck our heads out of the tank. More Electrode than I had ever seen had surrounded the tank. There were too many to count.

"The rancher starting blabbing about how the Electrode could blow away the town if they all exploded at once. I think he was just jealous that we were doing a better job than he was! But he had to get involved. And that goody-goody Ash tried to help, too."

"I remember," Jessie said. "Ash got Pikachu to attack us with Thundershock. That was hilarious! The attack had no effect because we fortified the Electrode Eliminator against electric attacks."

"I stepped on the gas," James said. "I wasn't going to let a bunch of overcharged Poké Balls get in our way. Then that rancher interfered. He turned his

vicious Diglett on us. He even called on Dugtrio, the evolved form of Diglett. The Diglett and Dugtrio dug a tunnel all around the tank. The Electrode Eliminator sank into the ground. Then the Diglett and Dugtrio kept on digging. We got carried away through their tunnels."

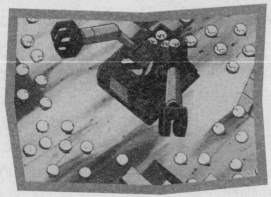

"Those worms can really move!" Meowth exclaimed.

"We fell out of the Electrode Eliminator," James remembered. "We landed in some kind of valley, and the tank was smashed to bits. The Electrode ended up there, too. The Diglett tunnels led to a place where the Electrode could live happily ever after, away from civilization."

"The Electrode didn't seem too happy to see us there," Meowth remembered, shuddering. "I felt like the bad end of a firecracker by the time they were done with us."

"Uh, James?" Jessie asked.

"Yes, Jess?"

"I thought you were trying to tell us a story about how we succeeded at something," Jessie said.

"That's right," James said. "That's the story of how we made an honest living by rounding up Electrode."

"But we didn't round up the Electrode!" Jessie yelled. "Instead, we got pummeled by some measly Diglett. Then the Electrode used us for exploding practice. Meowth's right. We failed. Just like we always do!"

James frowned. "I didn't think of it that way."

"We won't be thinking anything soon," Meowth said. "We're about to crash into the Savage Mountains!"

Jessie and James snapped to attention. They were right in the middle of the storm. Strong winds rocked the balloon back and forth. One more gust would send them crashing into the rocky peaks.

"What should we do?" James asked, panicked.

"Hold on!" Jessie yelled. Team Rocket held one another and closed their eyes.

Rain lashed at their faces. Another blast of wind kicked up. The Meowth balloon careened through the stormy sky.

Then, suddenly, the balloon stopped moving.

Jessie opened her eyes.

The balloon hadn't crashed. They had landed on top of a pointy rock.

"I think we're safe," Jessie said.

James and Meowth let go of each other. James walked to the edge of the balloon basket.

The Meowth balloon floated above them. There was a jagged tear in the balloon fabric, but nothing major. Jessie was right. They were safe.

James jumped for joy. "All right!" he yelled enthusiastically. "High five!"

Meowth and Jessie jumped up, ready to high-five James.

The balloon rocked.

"Uh-oh," Meowth said. "I think we might have made a wrong move."

The balloon basket began to slide off the rocky point.

"Come on, you blustering balloon," Jessie said. "Fly!"

But by this time, the hole in the fabric had let out all the air. The balloon lost its balance and plummeted to the ground below.

"Looks like Team Rocket's falling off again!" they all cried.

8

An Old Friend

For once, luck was on Team Rocket's side. The balloon could have crashed into the rocky ground at the foot of the mountain. Instead, it landed in a leafy treetop.

Meowth sighed with relief. "Our balloon's busted," said the Pokémon. "But we're not! Let's climb down. A magnificent Meowth like me shouldn't be perching like a Pidgeotto."

Branches scratched them as they scrambled down the tree trunk. Leaves poked them. Finally, they reached the ground.

"I'm so tired," Jessie said. "What time is it, anyway?"

James looked up at the night sky. A sliver of a moon lit up the darkness.

"It looks like it's time for bed," James said.

"I say it's time to eat!" said Meowth. "My poor stomach's as empty as James's head."

"I should fight you for that," James said. "But I'm too weak from hunger."

"Stop talking about how hungry you are," Jessie snapped. "I'm hungry, too, but you don't see me complaining. Besides, we've got to go back up those mountains and get that jeweled collar for the Boss."

"No way! I'm not getting anything for that pampered Persian until I get some grub," Meowth said.

James pointed into the distance. "Isn't that a Pokémon Center? They've got lots of food there."

Just ahead was a small town. Street-lights lit up the tree-lined streets. In the center of town rose a dome-shaped building topped with the letter P. At a Pokémon Center, Pokémon Trainers could get a good meal and a warm place to sleep. If their Pokémon needed healing, they'd get excellent care from Nurse Joy and Chansey, a pink Pokémon trained to heal other Pokémon.

Right now, the only thing Team Rocket was interested in was food.

Well, maybe not the only thing.

"Maybe we can catch some Pokémon for the Boss while we're there," James suggested. "He'll be so happy we'll never have to dig for clams again!"

"Food first," said Meowth. "I can't swipe Pokémon on an empty stomach."

Team Rocket headed for the Pokémon Center. The door was always open for Pokémon Trainers, no matter what time of night.

But Jessie, James, and Meowth were also Pokémon thieves. They snuck in through the back door. The hum

of the refrigerator led them to the kitchen.

"There's got to be something good here," Jessie whispered as she opened up the kitchen cabinets.

James searched every corner of the refrigerator but found nothing.

Meowth opened up a drawer. "Aha!" he said. "A whole carrot!"

Jessie and James rushed to Meowth's side. Jessie grabbed a kitchen knife.

"Perfect!" she said. "We'll divide it into three."

Meowth hugged the carrot. "Meowth found it, and Meowth's gonna eat it!"

Before Jessie and James could object, Meowth ran

out of the kitchen.

Jessie and James charged out the door. Meowth had vanished.

"Let's split up," Jessie suggested. "Meowth can't get far."

Jessie left James and turned down a dark hallway.

"Meowth!" she whispered harshly. "Turn over that carrot now!"

Suddenly, a small light appeared at the end of the hallway.

"Meowth," Jessie said. "Is that you?"

The light got closer, and Jessie realized it belonged to a flashlight – held by a Pokémon. The Pokémon had

an egg-shaped body that was pink on top and white on the bottom. It had two tiny hands, and white feathers on the sides of its body. Its pink ears looked like big ribbons curled on top of its head. A necklace hung around its neck.

"Blissey?" Jessie whispered in amazement. Jessie knew that Blissey was the evolved form of Chansey, the Egg Pokémon. But there was something familiar about this Blissey.

Blissey took a step closer. It seemed to know Jessie, too.

Blissey held up the necklace. Jessie could see a charm hanging from the chain. It looked like the top half of a broken egg.

Jessie reached into her pocket. She pulled out a charm that looked like the bottom half of a broken egg. She held it up to Blissey's charm.

The two pieces fit. A perfect match.

"It is you!" Jessie cried. She and Blissey hugged each other.

James and Meowth appeared in the hallway.

"What's all this?" Meowth asked. "Do you two know each other?"

Jessie nodded. "It was a long time ago...." she began.

9

Jessie and Blissey's Story

"The beautiful woman you see before you was once a beautiful young girl in pigtails," Jessie began.

"Beautiful woman? Where?" James asked.

Jessie ignored him. "I had a dream back then. I wanted to be a Nurse Pokémon more than anything."

"A Nurse Pokémon?" Meowth said. "Only Chansey can be Nurse Pokémon. Not humans."

"That's just what my grandfather said," Jessie replied. "He tried to discourage me. But I wanted it so much. He finally gave in, and I started my first day at

Chansey Nursing School.

"The teacher was Nurse Joy. All of the students were Chansey Pokémon except me. I knew it would be hard, but I didn't care. At first, I was a star pupil. I learned how to bandage patients. I learned the best kind of food to feed sick Pokémon.

"One Chansey was having trouble with its lessons. It kept getting tangled up in the bandages and dropping food on the floor. We were both outcasts in a way, and we became friends. I helped that Chansey study. We made a great team."

Blissey smiled as Jessie told the story.

"But Nurse Pokémon School got harder," Jessie continued. "Nurse Joy asked all the students to use the Pokémon ability called Sing to sing the patients to sleep. Chansey could do that easily. But I couldn't do it at all. The song made me fall asleep! I was a failure.

"I left the school before graduation. There was no point in staying. But Chansey made it! I watched her graduate through a window. Nurse Joy gave each Chansey a nurse's hat and an egg-shaped charm on a chain. I was happy for Chansey, but I couldn't bear to watch any longer. My dream was dashed. I walked away

from the school without looking back.

"Then Chansey ran up to me. It broke the egg in half and gave me the other piece. Even though I was leaving, I knew we would always be friends," Jessie said.

"*Blissey*," agreed Blissey.

James and Meowth were moved by the story. They hugged each other and cried.

"And now look at you!" Jessie told Blissey. "You're all grown up. You've even evolved into a Blissey. You must be doing great."

Blissey frowned and hung its head. *"Blissey blissey blissey."*

Meowth translated as the Pokémon spoke. "Blissey says that it still messes things up. Nurse Joy gets mad at Blissey sometimes."

James wiped a final tear from his eye and sighed. "Is this reunion over yet? We need to find food, remember?"

Blissey smiled. She began to chatter happily. *"Blissey! Blissey blissey bliss!"*

"Blissey says if we follow her, she can get us all the food we need," Meowth said.

"What are we waiting for?" James asked.

Team Rocket followed Blissey down the hall. Blissey opened a door and stepped inside.

She had led them into the food storage room. Boxes, cartons, bottles, and crates of food filled the shelves.

"This place is a paradise for a famished feline like me," said Meowth.

Blissey packed up all the food and carried it outside.

Jessie hugged Blissey. "I almost feel bad taking all this," she said. "Are you sure it's all right?"

"Don't ask questions," Meowth said.

"Meowth's right. There's only one question worth asking," James said.

"What's that?" asked Jessie.

James grinned. "When do we eat?"

10

Team Rocket to the Rescue

By the next morning, Jessie, James, and Meowth were feeling pretty good. The night before, they had eaten a big dinner. They got a great night's sleep. After a good breakfast, they fixed the balloon and loaded it up with the remaining crates of food.

"We'll never go hungry again," Meowth said happily as they lifted off above the trees. "It's a good thing we ran into your old friend Blissey."

Jessie focused her binoculars as they slowly drifted past the Pokémon Center. "I wish I could say good-bye," Jessie said. "But I can't let Nurse Joy know that Blissey and I are friends. Nurse Pokémon aren't supposed to associate with criminals like me."

Then Jessie spotted Blissey through a window in the Pokémon Center. Nurse Joy was frowning and talking to Blissey. The Happiness Pokémon hung its head, and tears ran down its pink cheeks. Behind them, a security video showed Blissey carrying food out of the storage room.

And that wasn't all. Watching the scene were Ash, Misty, Brock, and Pikachu.

"Oh, no!" said Jessie.

"What's the matter?" James asked.

Jessie lowered the binoculars. "It's double trouble," she replied. "Blissey got caught on camera taking the food for us. And that Goody Two-Shoes, Ash, is there with his friends."

"Great! We can steal Pikachu," Meowth said.

"We can't think about that now," said Jessie. "We have to help Blissey. I wish it wasn't too late to take back the food."

"I have an idea," James said. "We could pretend we spooked Blissey and made it give us the food."

"Great idea!" said Meowth.

Jessie faced her friends. "You'll really help me? I know how much this food means to you."

"One of your friends is in danger," James said. "Of course we'll help."

Jessie smiled. "Then let's do it!"

Meowth steered the balloon in front of the Pokémon Center. Jessie and James packed the food into a net and carefully lowered it to the ground. The balloon landed alongside the net.

There was no response from the Pokémon Center,

so James grabbed a megaphone.

"Ahem," James cleared his throat. "Oh, no. What should we do with all the food we stole from the Pokémon Center?"

The doors swung open. Nurse Joy and Blissey stepped outside, followed by Ash and his friends. Blissey smiled at Jessie and started to wave, but Jessie put a finger to her lips to keep Blissey quiet. Blissey had to go along with the plan so it would work.

"Team Rocket!" Ash shouted.

"So you're the ones who stole all the provisions," Nurse Joy said.

"It's true," Jessie said.

"We, Team Rocket, scared Blissey into doing it for us," James added.

"We forced Blissey to do it against its will," said Meowth.

Ash glared at them. "Thanks to you, we didn't get any breakfast! Give back that food right now."

Jessie thought for a second. "I'll tell you what. We'll give back the food if you give us all the Pokémon in the center."

"I can't do that," Nurse Joy said.

"Then I guess you'll all have to go hungry," Jessie said.

Just then, Blissey stepped in front of Nurse Joy. The Pokémon seemed confused by Jessie's actions. She took another step closer.

"Stay away," Jessie whispered.

But Blissey kept coming.

"No, no," Jessie hissed. "You're a Nurse Pokémon. It wouldn't look right for you to be friends with a member of the evil Team Rocket."

Blissey smiled. It didn't care if Jessie was a member of Team Rocket. All it knew was that Jessie was its friend.

"Blissey, what are you doing?" Nurse Joy asked.

Jessie panicked. She couldn't let Nurse Joy know the truth. Blissey might lose its job.

There was only one thing to do.

"Lickitung! Arbok!" Jessie yelled as she threw two Poké Balls. "Stop that do-gooding little Blissey!"

Blasting Off Again!

The two Poké Balls burst open. Lickitung, a large pink Pokémon, came out of first. Lickitung walked on two sturdy legs, had black, beady eyes, and a long, sticky tongue that it used for its attacks.

The second Pokémon, Arbok, was purple and very large. Arbok's poison attacks could paralyze its opponents.

The two scary-looking Pokémon couldn't frighten Blissey. It kept walking toward Jessie.

"Oh, no!" Misty cried. "Blissey is in trouble. What is it thinking?"

"It looks like its trying to recover the stolen food all

by itself," said Brock.

Jessie tried to keep from smiling. Her plan was working perfectly.

Suddenly, Arbok leaped through the air toward Blissey. Lickitung stomped behind.

Jessie had forgotten to tell them about her plan!

Lickitung slammed into Blissey with all its weight. Then Arbok wrapped its long, powerful body around the pink-and-white Pokémon.

"That's too much!" Jessie whispered frantically. "Just pretend attack. Pretend!"

Arbok let go of its grip on Blissey. The Nurse Pokémon kept walking toward Jessie. Blissey still didn't understand what its friend was doing.

"Blissey is being so brave," Misty said.

"Lickitung, Slap!" Jessie commanded her Pokémon. Then she whispered, "Fake it."

Lickitung ran up behind Blissey. It picked up the Nurse Pokémon with its long tongue.

Then it placed Blissey gently back on the ground.

"Arbok! Fang!" Jessie yelled. Then she whispered, "You fake it, too."

Arbok jumped up and bared its sharp fangs. It aimed right for Blissey's neck.

Then it stopped in midair. Its fangs just missed

puncturing Blissey's skin.

"How do you like that, Blissey?" Jessie jeered. "That's what happens when you take on Team Rocket." It hurt Jessie to say such mean words, but it was for Blissey's own good.

Blissey didn't seem to care how angry Jessie was. It wouldn't turn back.

"Stay away, Blissey. I mean it," Jessie said. She looked at Ash. Normally that half-pint hero would be interfering by now.

"Don't just sit there gawking, you twerp," Jessie told Ash. "Come help Blissey."

"I was just about to," Ash said. "Pikachu, go!"

"I'm tired of waiting," James said. "If you won't come to us, we'll come to you!"

Meowth hit a button on a remote control. Two mechanical arms reached out of the remote control box and grabbed Pikachu. The arms held Pikachu high in the air.

Pikachu frowned. Sparks danced on its red cheeks.

"Get back, Blissey," Jessie whispered. "Trust me."

Blissey stepped away from the balloon.

"Pikachuuuuuuuuuu!" The yellow Pokémon exploded

with a Thunder attack. The electric charge raced down the metal arms. It ripped through Jessie, James, and Meowth.

The mechanical arm opened. Pikachu jumped to safety. Then it grabbed Blissey's hand. Together they ran back to Ash and the others.

"Good work, Pikachu," Ash said.

Nurse Joy hugged Blissey. "Forgive me for doubting you. You're the best Nurse Pokémon I could ever want."

Blissey turned and looked at Jessie. Jessie winked.

Blissey smiled. It finally understood.

"It's the best way," Jessie whispered. "I'll never forget you."

James nudged Jessie. "Now that Blissey is all right, we should make our getaway. There's no reason why we still can't take the food."

"Right," Jessie said. "So long!"

"Oh, no, you don't," Ash said. "We still didn't get any breakfast."

Ash threw two Poké Balls.

"Squirtle! Chikorita!" Ash called out as the balls opened.

Squirtle, a Water-type Pokémon, had a shell on its back. Chikorita was one of Ash's newest Pokémon. It looked like a yellow banana with four legs, big red eyes, and a green leaf on top of its head. A ring of shiny green circles dotted Chikorita's neck.

"Get that food back," Ash told them.

"Arbok, Lickitung, fight back!" Jessie said.

Arbok and Lickitung charged at Ash's Pokémon. Pikachu quickly jolted Arbok with an electric shock. Chikorita used an attack called Vine Whip on Lickitung. Green vines shot out of two of the circles around Chikorita's neck. The vines lashed around Lickitung's tail. The Chikorita picked up Lickitung and slammed it into the ground.

Ash gave one last command. "Squirtle, Water Gun!"

Squirtle's mouth opened, and a powerful jet of water blasted out, knocking over Lickitung and Arbok. The Pokémon were pushed back into the Team Rocket balloon. Squirtle's Water Gun got stronger. The water slammed into the balloon, sending it flying across the sky.

"We may be blasting off," Team Rocket said, "but we've still got the food!" The net holding the crates dangled below the balloon.

"Chikorita, Razor Leaf!" Ash cried.

The leaf on top of Chikorita's head swirled, and two sharp leaves flew out. The leaves sliced through

the net, and the crates of food dropped safely to the ground.

The sudden loss of weight sent the balloon spiraling through the air.

"It looks like we really are blasting off!" Team Rocket yelled.

The balloon zoomed through the sky as though it had been shot by a slingshot. Finally, it stopped in midair and then crashed onto a grassy field below.

Dazed, Jessie, James, and Meowth climbed out of the balloon basket.

"What happened?" asked James.

"Who am I?" asked Meowth, holding its head.

"You're a failure," Jessie said. "Just like the rest of us. We can't even steal food from a Pokémon Center. We'll never be any good at anything!"

"Don't be silly, Jess," James said. "We didn't fail today."

"We didn't?" Jessie asked.

"The blue-haired bumbler is right," Meowth said. "We didn't fail. You wanted to make Blissey look good, didn't ya? Well, Nurse Joy thinks Blissey is a hero. You wanted to save Blissey, and we did. We're a success!"

Jessie let the words sink in. Then she grinned.

"We did succeed, didn't we!" she said. "We're not failures."

Jessie whacked James on the back of the head. "Don't you ever call us failures again."

"But, Jess, it was you —" James began.

"This calls for a celebration," Jessie said. "Meowth, do you still have that carrot?"

Meowth held it up. "Right here."

"Then it's Carrot Surprise for everybody," Jessie said.

"What's the surprise?" James asked.

Just then, a beeping sound came from a machine inside the balloon.

"Here's a surprise we don't want," said Meowth. "The Boss!"

Giovanni appeared on a videophone screen. His face looked beet red.

"What happened to you good-for-nothing Pokémon thieves?" the Boss asked. "Persian needs its collar. I can't believe you messed up such a simple errand. When I get through with you —"

Jessie clicked off the videophone.

"He was spoiling our celebration," Jessie said. "We'll

deal with him later. We'll get through it."

"We always do," said James.

"That's 'cause we stick together," added Meowth.

Jessie smiled. "Now *that's* what I call success!"